Here's what kids, parents, and teachers have to say to Ron Roy, author of the A to Z Mysteries series:

"I've read all of your books and enjoyed them so much I can't pick a favorite! When my 6-year-old sister starts reading more complicated chapter books, I'll tell her she should read your books!"—Elizabeth P.

"I like your books because they keep me on the edge of my chair."—Sierra M.

"I love your books *sooooooo* much! My mom can't buy them fast enough. I always have my nose in a book now!"—Esther K.

"Your books are the coolest. I wish there were 1,000 letters in the alphabet!"—Laura T.

"I can't thank you enough for opening up the world of books to my son."—Emily W.

"As a teacher, I want to thank you for creating material that is so age-appropriate and so engaging for the studen[ts] makes teaching readin[g] —Shirley K[

This book is dedicated to teachers everywhere.
—R.R.

To my wonderful, super-cool Molly
—J.S.G.

ISBN 0-439-62177-1

Text copyright © 2003 by Ron Roy.
Illustrations copyright © 2003 by John Steven Gurney.
All rights reserved.
Published by Scholastic Inc., 557 Broadway, New York, NY 10012,
by arrangement with Random House Children's Books,
a division of Random House, Inc.
SCHOLASTIC and associated logos are trademarks and/or
registered trademarks of Scholastic Inc.

20 19 18 17 16 15 14   8 9/0

Printed in the U.S.A   40

First Scholastic printing, February 2004

A to Z MYSTERIES is a registered trademark of Random House, Inc.

A to Z Mysteries

The Talking T. Rex

by Ron Roy

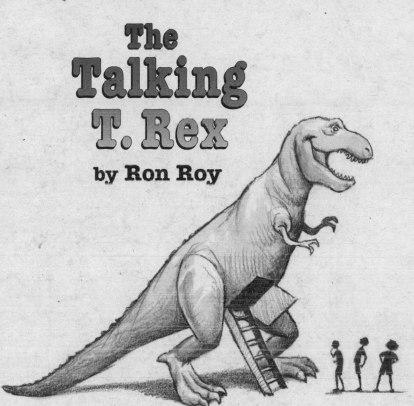

illustrated by
John Steven Gurney

SCHOLASTIC INC.

New York Toronto London Auckland Sydney
Mexico City New Delhi Hong Kong Buenos Aires

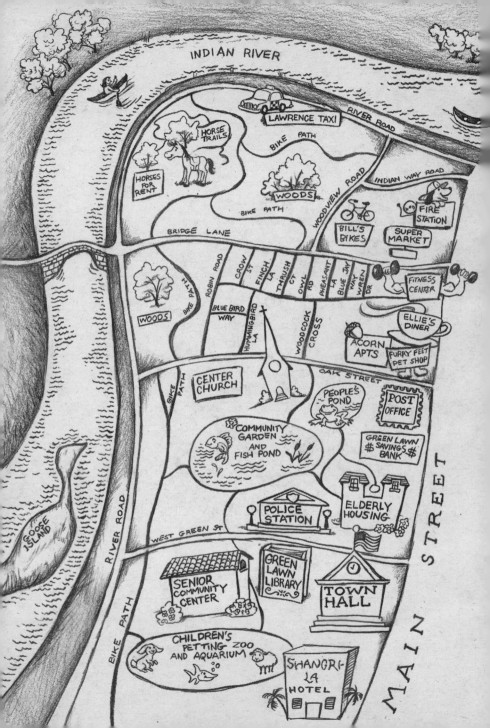

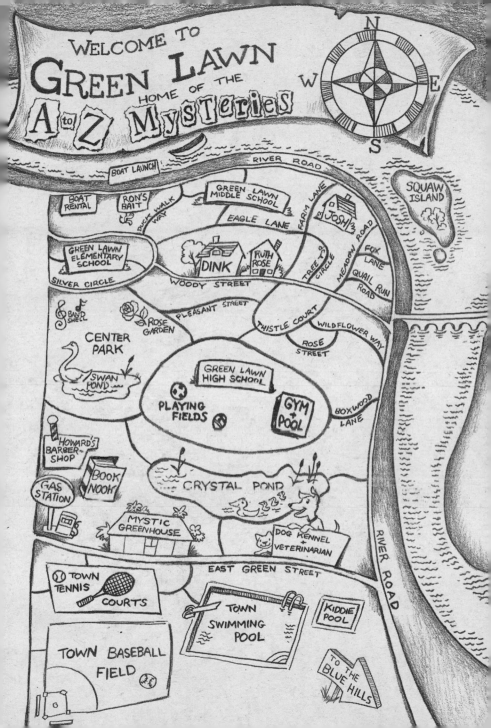

CHAPTER 1

Dink, Josh, and Ruth Rose hurried toward the high school. It was July 3, so they all wore shorts and T-shirts. Josh's dog, Pal, was leading the way on his leash. His floppy ears nearly touched the ground as he sniffed everything in his path.

"I can't wait to see Jud again," Dink said. Dink's full name was Donald David Duncan, but most people called him Dink.

The three kids had met Jud Wheat when they visited his parents' dude ranch in Montana. When Josh found a huge gold nugget there, he gave it to Jud to help pay for college. Now Jud was coming to Green Lawn for a visit.

"I wonder what the big surprise is that he mentioned in his postcard," Ruth Rose said. She liked to wear one color. Today it was dark blue, from her headband down to her sneakers. The color matched her sharp blue eyes.

"Read it to us," Josh said to Dink.

Dink pulled a postcard from his pocket. He read it out loud as they stopped at Pleasant Street:

Hi, Dink, Josh, and Ruth Rose,
I'll be in Green Lawn on July 3 with
a huge surprise. Meet me at the high
school grounds at noon. Bye for now.
Your friend,
Jud

"Maybe the surprise is a large pizza," Josh said.

"You wish," Ruth Rose said.

"Look, there's Mr. Pocket," Dink said, turning toward Center Park. Their friend Thaddeus Pocket was standing in the town rose garden. He wore work gloves and held a shovel. His dog, Randolph, was gazing at the ducks in Swan Pond.

Josh dropped the leash, and Pal ran over to greet the fluffy little dog.

"Hi, Mr. Pocket!" Ruth Rose said.

"Well, hello, kiddos," the white-haired man said. "All set for the fireworks tomorrow night? I noticed workers setting up near the swimming pool."

"We're all going," Josh said. "Will you and Randolph be there?"

"I will," Mr. Pocket said. "But old Randolph prefers to stay home. He doesn't like the big booms."

"Pal is staying home, too," Josh said. "He doesn't even like birthday candles!"

Mr. Pocket started digging up a

dead-looking rosebush that had no leaves or blossoms on it. In a wheel-barrow was a healthy bush, this one covered with shiny green leaves.

"Want to help me plant this new one?" Mr. Pocket asked the kids.

Dink looked at his watch. "Okay, but then we have to meet a friend at the high school. His name is Jud Wheat, and he's studying to become a teacher."

"He brought a surprise all the way from Montana!" Ruth Rose said.

"This won't take long at all," Mr. Pocket said. He assigned tasks as he removed the old rosebush.

Ruth Rose poured a handful of fertil-izer into the hole.

Dink shoveled in some of the loose soil.

Josh used the garden hose to fill the hole with water.

"Mother Nature may give us some rain by tonight," Mr. Pocket said, glancing up at the clouds. He lifted the new bush out of the wheelbarrow and placed it in the hole. He made sure the plant stood up straight.

"That looks splendid," Mr. Pocket said. "You three are super gardeners. Dink, if you'll return the wheelbarrow to the shed, I'll fill in the rest of the soil."

Dink handed Mr. Pocket the shovel and steered the wheelbarrow over to a garden shed. An old screwdriver held the door closed. Dink opened the door and guided the wheelbarrow inside.

There was barely room for the wheelbarrow in the packed little shed. The shelves were a jumble of pots, jars, bags of fertilizer, pails, books about gardening, and tools like the ones Dink's parents owned. On the clean brick floor were rakes, shovels, gardening stakes, and coiled hoses.

Dink left the wheelbarrow leaning

against a stack of empty burlap bags at the rear of the shed. He replaced the screwdriver and left.

Just as Dink reached the others, a red car turned off Main Street and drove toward the high school. Steam escaped from under the car's hood.

"Is that your friend?" Mr. Pocket asked. "I hope he didn't drive all the way from Montana in that thing!"

"We'd better go," Dink said. "Want to meet Jud, Mr. Pocket?"

"Not right now," Mr. Pocket said. "Randolph and I need our lunch and a nap. Thanks for your help."

The kids took Pal and ran toward the red car. It stopped and a tall young man got out. He had dark, curly hair and broad shoulders. He was wearing a T-shirt, cutoff jeans, and red high-top sneakers.

"That's not Jud," Dink said as they approached the man.

CHAPTER 2

The man turned and waved. "Hi. You must be Dink, Josh, and Ruth Rose. I'm Scoop Raker. I work with Jud and his friend Dean. They should be here any minute."

Scoop raised the hood of his car, and more steam billowed out. He took a jug of water from the front seat, then unscrewed the radiator cap. Suddenly he yelled and stuck his finger in his mouth.

"You'd think I'd learn by now," Scoop said, shaking his head. He pulled a Band-Aid from his pocket, removed

the covering, and wrapped the green Band-Aid around his finger.

Just then a long flatbed truck pulled up alongside Scoop's car. A brown tarp covered the truck bed, concealing something big and lumpy. The whole thing was tied down with ropes.

The driver's door opened and a tall, lanky guy hopped to the ground. He was

wearing jeans, a short-sleeve shirt, and a cowboy hat. "Howdy," the man said, beaming at Dink, Josh, and Ruth Rose.

"Hi, Jud!" they all said at once.

A man stepped out of the passenger's side of the truck. He was short and wiry and had black hair tied in a ponytail. He wore work boots, baggy shorts, and a flannel shirt with the sleeves ripped off.

"Guys, I'd like you to meet my roommate and best friend, Dean Whitefeather," Jud said. "Dean, this is Dink, Josh, and Ruth Rose."

Dean walked around the truck toward the kids. He had a friendly smile and dark eyes. His shirt pocket was filled with pens. A ring of keys on his belt jangled when he walked.

The kids shook hands with Dean. Then Jud and Dean made a fuss over Pal, who gave them both big, wet kisses.

"Well, what say we get busy?" Dean said, glancing at the sky. "Rain by midnight, I'll bet." He started untying the ropes.

Scoop climbed back into his car. "I passed the hotel on the way in," he said. "I'll go check on our room." He drove away, with only a little steam escaping from under the hood.

"Can we help?" Ruth Rose asked.

Dean smiled at her. "My three favorite words," he said.

"You guys can coil these ropes as we untie them," Jud said. "Just lay 'em on the ground."

Josh told Pal to stay, and the kids pitched in. After a few minutes, the ropes had all been removed. Dean and

Jud yanked the tarp to the ground.

When Dink saw what had made all those lumps, he jumped back. He was staring right at the head of a Tyrannosaurus rex!

"Meet Tyrone the Tyrannosaurus," laughed Jud. "He looks even better when he's not in pieces."

Dink gulped. "Where did you get it?" he asked.

"We bought him," Jud said.

Josh grinned. "From a dinosaur store?" he joked.

"No, from the man who built Tyrone," Dean said. "He planned to start a dinosaur theme park, but he lost interest. He put an ad in the paper, and we saw it and bought Tyrone and the truck."

"Um, why do you need a dinosaur?" Ruth Rose asked.

"To raise money," Jud said. "Dean and I want to teach kids about the dinosaurs that used to live in Montana. We've decided to build a little museum on a piece of land behind the dude ranch."

"And Tyrone will be the star attraction," Dean added.

"When we first saw Tyrone, he was in the guy's barn all in pieces like you see him now. I developed a computer program to make him move and talk. We make money by taking him around the country and collecting donations."

"Is Scoop a teacher, too?" asked Dink.

"No, we met Scoop in Wyoming. He was looking for work, so we hired him," Jud said. "He's in charge of hotel rooms, getting permission for us to set up outside schools, making the flyers, stuff like that. Scoop wants to work at the museum once it's built."

Dean climbed up onto the truck bed. "Let's put this guy back together, Jud," he said.

"How do you put him together?" Dink asked.

"Easy, like building a model with an Erector set," Dean said. He pointed to a box of large nuts, bolts, and cables on the truck bed.

"What's Tyrone made of?" Ruth Rose asked. "Is he heavy?"

"Not really," Jud said. He took the Tyrannosaurus's tail from Dean and laid it gently on the ground.

"Tyrone's mostly fiberglass and rubber. His bones are aluminum. The teeth, toenails, and eyes are plastic."

The kids gently touched one of the six-inch-long teeth. "It looks so real!" Josh said.

"Careful, some of those edges are sharp," Dean said. He grinned and wiggled a finger that was wrapped in a green Band-Aid.

They all looked over when Scoop's red car zoomed up. Scoop parked the car and climbed out with a stack of papers in his hand.

"How'd you kids like to help out?" he asked. "Can you take these flyers around town?"

Scoop handed the flyers to Ruth Rose. She looked at the top one. Beneath a picture of a Tyrannosaurus were the words:

COME MEET TYRONE THE TALKING

TYRANNOSAURUS!

BEHIND THE HIGH SCHOOL, JULY **4**,

AT NOON. ONE-DOLLAR DONATION

PER CUSTOMER REQUESTED!

"You three will get in free, of course," Jud said, looking over Ruth Rose's shoulder.

"Cool!" Josh said.

"Who should we give them to?" Dink asked.

"Anyone and everyone," Scoop said. "Stores, friends, anyone who likes dinosaurs."

Ruth Rose divided the stack of flyers into three smaller piles. They each took a pile.

"Will you guys watch Pal?" Josh asked.

"No problem," Scoop said.

The kids headed toward Main Street with their flyers.

An hour later, the kids were back. "The whole *town* is coming to see Tyrone tomorrow!" Dink said.

"Excellent! So what do you think of him now?" Jud asked, pointing to Tyrone.

Tyrone stood balanced on his thick rear legs and tail. His body and tail stretched out longer than a school bus, and he was nearly as tall as Dink's house. His back feet were as long as Pal, who was sniffing a giant plastic toenail.

"It's . . . it's . . ." Dink couldn't find the right words.

Jud and Dean laughed.

"Tyrone isn't full-sized," Dean said. "An adult T. rex would be even bigger. Come on, I'll show you what's inside this guy's belly."

He unclipped his keys and inserted one of them into a little hole in Tyrone's side. When Dean turned the key, a small metal ring popped out. Dean pulled on the ring and a door swung open on hinges.

"Awesome!" Josh said. "It was totally hidden!"

Dean picked up a rubber wedge from inside and used it to hold the door open. Then he reached through the doorway and pulled down a set of folded, hinged steps. "Have a look," he said.

The kids kneeled on the stairs and peered inside the dinosaur's belly. Aluminum bars supported the walls. A row of hooks held tools and coils of rope and wire. There were no windows, and it was hot inside.

The floor was partly covered by a piece of carpet. A laptop computer sat on a small table in the middle of the carpet. A bunch of gray computer cables snaked across the floor. A few of the cables climbed up the dinosaur's chest and disappeared inside its neck and head.

"The computer does everything,"

Dean said. "I can move Tyrone's tail, mouth, and front feet just by clicking the mouse."

He squeezed by the kids and stepped inside Tyrone's belly. "I've put a loudspeaker up in Tyrone's head," Dean explained. He showed them a small microphone. "I speak into this, and it sounds like the voice is coming from Tyrone's mouth."

"Can you make him talk now?" Josh asked.

"That'll have to wait till tomorrow," Dean said. "We've been on the road since about five this morning, and I'm pretty whipped. I need about ten hours of sleep!"

Dean and the kids climbed out of Tyrone's belly, and he closed the door.

"Are you all staying at the Shangri-la?" Ruth Rose asked.

"Jud and Scoop are," Dean said. "I'm going to bed down out here." He pulled a sleeping bag from inside the truck and dropped it on the ground.

"Why do you sleep outside?" Dink asked.

Dean grinned. "Those two snore," he said, gesturing toward Scoop and Jud. "Besides, I like sleeping under the stars. Plus, I guard Tyrone. In the morning I'll go to the hotel and use their shower."

"Where can we get some good burgers?" Scoop asked the kids. "And breakfast tomorrow?"

"Ellie's Diner!" all three kids said.

Ruth Rose pointed toward Main Street. "It's between the pet shop and the fitness center," she said.

"Thanks for your help. We'll see you tomorrow," Jud said.

The three men climbed into the red car and Scoop drove off toward Main Street. A rumble of thunder over their heads sent the kids running for home.

CHAPTER 3

Thunder woke Dink during the night. He lay snugly in bed, watching the storm through his window. As lightning flashed, he thought about Tyrone, standing out there in the dark and rain.

The next day Dink got to the high school around eleven-thirty. He gazed up at Tyrone. The dinosaur was tall and silent under a blue sky. His mouth was closed and his eyes stared into the distance. The grass was still wet from the storm, and mist rose as it dried in the sun.

Jud, Dean, and Scoop were nowhere in sight. Dink walked over to the truck and looked in the window. Dean's sleeping bag was spread across the seats.

A few minutes later, Ruth Rose showed up with her little brother, Nate. She was dressed in orange, from her headband down to her socks and sneakers.

When Nate saw Tyrone, his mouth fell open. He walked up to one of the rear legs and touched it. "It feels like a rubber dinosaur toy," he said.

Josh and his brothers, Brian and Bradley, came loping across the playing field. Pal was tugging on his leash.

The twins stopped in their tracks. "It's a Tankosaurus!" Brian yelled.

"No it's not!" Bradley argued. "It's a Trainosaurus!"

Josh laughed. "Guys, it's a Ty-ran-no-saur-us."

"It's not real, is it, Josh?" asked Bradley.

Josh let Pal off his leash. "No," he said. "It's just a big action figure."

Scoop pulled up in his red car and parked next to Tyrone. He hopped out and walked over to the kids.

"Morning," he said. "Some storm last night, huh? The thunder nearly knocked us out of our beds."

Scoop sat on the ground and pulled on a pair of sandals. His wet sneakers were tied together, hanging from the car's antenna.

Dean and Jud came walking through Center Park.

"Hi, kids," Jud said. "Scoop, you missed a great breakfast. That Ellie makes amazing waffles!"

Scoop nodded. "I couldn't seem to wake up," he said.

Jud looked at Nate, Brian, and Bradley. "Do you guys like dinosaurs?"

The three little kids beamed and nodded.

"T. rex is my favorite!" Nate said.

People from town began arriving and stood around gaping up at Tyrone. Dink waved to Mr. Paskey from the Book Nook. He saw Mr. and Mrs. Spivets, who owned the Shangri-la Hotel.

Dink saw his mom show up with Josh's and Ruth Rose's mothers. Josh's mom carried a picnic basket.

"Guys, go sit with Mom, okay?" Josh asked the twins.

"Can we take Pal?" Brian asked.

Josh handed the leash over to Brian. "Okay, but don't let him off. And take him home when Mom leaves, okay?"

"Why does Brian get to do everything?" Bradley whined.

Josh sighed. "You two can share the leash, okay?"

Nate, Brian, and Bradley led Pal toward their mothers.

"This is great," Jud said, watching the crowd increase. "Dean, why don't you get Tyrone ready while Scoop and I collect money?"

While the kids were picking a place to sit, Dink saw more people he knew from town. A bunch of the O'Leary kids showed up, and Dink waved at them. Some people brought chairs or blankets to sit on. The high school playing field was filling up.

Jud and Scoop passed through the crowd, collecting a dollar from each person. When their hands were filled with bills, the men walked over to the truck and locked the money inside the cab. They each did this two or three times.

"They must make a ton of money," Josh said. "I'll bet there are two hundred people here!"

Jud climbed up onto the truck bed with a cordless microphone. "Thanks for coming, folks!" he said to the crowd.

When everyone was quiet, Jud went on to explain why they were raising money. "Our museum should be built by next summer, and I hope some of you will come for a visit," he said.

Jud pointed his mike at the dinosaur. "Now I'd like you all to meet my friend Tyrone. Tyrone, why don't you tell these good folks about yourself?" he said.

Nothing happened. Tyrone stood silent and still. He didn't say a word.

"I guess Tyrone is shy this morning," Jud said. Then, in a louder voice, he said, "Tyrone? Can you say hi to all our friends out here? Wiggle your tail if you hear me."

This got a few laughs, but Tyrone still didn't move.

Some of the kids in the audience began to fidget. A boy sitting behind Dink muttered, "I wonder if we can get our money back."

Then, suddenly, Tyrone's tail moved to the right, then to the left. His small front arms waved up and down. His mouth opened and Tyrone said, "Hi!" in a deep voice.

"HI, TYRONE!" the crowd yelled back.

"How many of you know what kind of dinosaur I am?" Tyrone asked. Dink recognized Dean's voice coming from Tyrone's mouth.

Every kid and adult raised a hand. "Tyrannosaurus!" Nate hollered.

"That's right, I'm a Tyrannosaurus rex," Tyrone said.

"Now, how many of you remembered to eat a good breakfast this morning?"

Most people raised a hand.

"Well," Tyrone said, nodding his massive head, "about seventy million years ago, *I* ate other dinosaurs for *my* breakfast!"

Everyone laughed.

Jud hopped off the truck and sat with Dink, Josh, and Ruth Rose.

"Dean's good with the crowd, isn't he?" Jud said.

"You'd swear Tyrone is really talking," Dink said.

Jud nodded. "Yeah, Dean's a genius with anything mechanical. He had me scared at the beginning, though. I thought something went wrong with the computer."

Tyrone told the audience all about the dinosaurs who once roamed North America. He talked about what they ate, how they protected themselves, and how they raised their young.

The show lasted about half an hour. "I hope you'll all go to the library and learn more about dinosaurs," Tyrone said, waving good-bye with his small arms. "And come visit me next summer in Montana!"

A lot of the kids yelled, "Bye, Tyrone!" as the people began to leave.

"That was so cool!" Josh told Jud. "How many schools have you gone to so far?"

Jud scratched his head. "Gosh, I don't really know, maybe fifty or so. Scoop keeps track of all that. I think he's lined up about twenty more before we head back to Montana."

Dean climbed out of Tyrone and walked over to where the kids and Jud were sitting.

"That was great," Jud told Dean. "But what happened at the beginning?"

Dean shrugged. "I couldn't get the laptop to boot up," he said. "One of the cables was loose."

"Well, at least you fixed it," Jud said, standing up. "It's getting warm," he added. "I could use some ice cream. After we clean up, why don't we meet at Ellie's? Tyrone is treating!"

"You just made Josh happy," Ruth Rose said. "What can we do?"

Jud pulled a plastic bag from his pocket. "If you'll go around and pick up paper, that would be a great help," he said.

While Jud walked toward the truck, Dink, Josh, and Ruth Rose spread out and began collecting litter.

Dink was leaning over to grab a crumpled flyer when he heard a shout. He looked up. The yell had come from near Tyrone. Jud, Dean, and Scoop were huddled in front of the open door.

Even from a hundred feet away, Dink could hear Jud yell, "I don't believe it!"

CHAPTER 4

Dink, Josh, and Ruth Rose ran toward Tyrone. "What happened?" Dink asked.

"Our money got stolen—that's what happened!" Scoop said.

"The money you just collected?" Josh asked.

Jud shook his head. "No, I still have that." He held up two thick stacks of bills with rubber bands around them. "I was going to add it to the rest of the money, but it's gone!"

Dean pointed to the floor inside Tyrone's belly. The table, chair, and carpet had been moved. Where the table and chair had stood was a square hole cut into the flooring. A hinged door was open, revealing a compartment. It was empty.

"I built that as a hiding place," Dean said. "That's where we kept the money, in a duffel bag. We've been putting it in there since we left Montana."

"How much money was there?" Josh asked.

Jud's face was white. "All the money we've made so far," he said in a shaky voice. "Almost five thousand dollars."

Six pairs of eyes stared into the empty compartment.

"I don't see when anyone could have gotten in there," Scoop said.

Jud closed his eyes for a second. "I put the duffel bag in there yesterday," he said, "after we got Tyrone all set up."

"So someone stole it between yesterday afternoon and this morning," Dean said. "And it couldn't have happened last night, because I slept out here."

"I'm going to get Officer Fallon!" Ruth Rose said. "He's the chief of police."

"What can he do now?" Jud asked. "The money is long gone."

"Officer Fallon catches a lot of crooks," Dink said.

Josh glanced down at the ground, dry now from the sun. "He might find some clues around here."

"They're right about bringing the police in, Jud," Dean said. "We have to do everything we can to find our money."

"I'll be right back!" Ruth Rose said as she took off running.

"Well, no one's getting *this* money," Jud said. He opened his shirt and stuffed the bills inside.

Dink felt Josh pinching his arm. When Dink looked at him, Josh motioned with his head for Dink to walk away with him.

He followed Josh away from the three men.

"I hate to say this," Josh whispered,

"but I think one of them stole the money." He tipped his chin toward Jud, Dean, and Scoop.

"Why would they do it?" Dink asked. "Jud and Dean really want to build the museum. And Scoop's going to work there. They wouldn't steal their own money, Josh."

"But who else has a key to the door or knows about that hiding place inside Tyrone?" Josh insisted.

Dink shook his head. He kicked a small stone. "No one can make me believe Jud would do such a rotten thing," he said.

Just then Ruth Rose and Officer Fallon came hurrying across Center Park. Dink and Josh walked back to the dinosaur.

Officer Fallon introduced himself and pulled his notebook and pen from a shirt pocket. "Ruth Rose told me what happened," he said. He looked at the three men. "May I have your names, please?"

He wrote down each name. "Scoop?" he asked. "Is that a nickname?"

Scoop grinned. "Yeah, I was the editor of my college newspaper. I got the name because I was always first with a news scoop. My real name is Michael Raker."

Officer Fallon wrote it down. "Can you show me where the money was when you fellas last saw it?"

Dean pointed through the door at the empty compartment. "It was in there, except when we were on the road. Then we kept it with us in the truck."

"I put the duffel inside that compartment yesterday afternoon," Jud said. "That's the last time I saw it."

"Wouldn't it be safer to keep your money in a bank?" Officer Fallon asked.

"We thought the money was safe inside the dinosaur," Jud said. "No one but us knew about the hidden compartment. And I was planning on taking the money to my bank back in Montana."

"Was that compartment locked?" the police chief asked, writing in his notebook.

Jud shook his head. "No, but we always keep this outer door locked."

Officer Fallon examined the keyhole. He removed the rubber wedge and swung the door back and forth on its hinges. "Who has keys to this door?"

"I have one," Dean said. He tapped his key ring.

Jud held up his keys. "And I have the only other key," he said.

Officer Fallon made another note on his pad. "So Mr. Wheat put the money into that compartment yesterday afternoon," he said. "Then this morning, after the show, Mr. Whitefeather looked for the money and discovered that it was gone. Is that correct?"

"Actually, no," Dean said. "I did the show, but it was Jud who found out the money was missing."

"Could the money have been stolen last night?" Officer Fallon said. "Where did you fellows sleep?"

"Scoop and I slept at the hotel," Jud said. "We left the money in the compartment. We always do. Dean sleeps outside. He likes to guard Tyrone."

Officer Fallon looked confused. "Who's Tyrone?" he asked.

"That's what we call the dinosaur," Scoop explained.

Officer Fallon glanced at Dean. "You slept out here all night?" he asked. "Even during the rain?"

Dean smiled. "No, when it started to rain, I took my sleeping bag into the truck."

Officer Fallon made more notes on his pad, then turned to Jud. "Could anyone have snuck into your room and taken your key while you slept?" he asked.

Jud shook his head. "The door was locked."

Officer Fallon looked at Dean. "How about your key, Mr. Whitefeather?" he asked. "Where was it while you slept out here?"

Dean held up his key ring. "Clipped to my belt, inside my sleeping bag with me."

Officer Fallon swung the door wide and looked at the computer. "Who makes this thing work?" he asked.

"I do," Dean said. "And my computer."

"So as far as you knew, the duffel bag was still hidden under the floor this morning," Officer Fallon stated.

"That's right," said Dean.

Officer Fallon peered inside Tyrone.

"And you would have been sitting right over the money at your computer, right, Mr. Whitefeather?"

Dean nodded. "But I figure it was already stolen by then," he said. "After the show, when Jud moved the table and pulled the rug back, the duffel bag was gone."

Officer Fallon placed the wedge so that the door remained slightly open. He looked at the three men. "Gentlemen, let's walk across the street to my office. I'd like you to think about everything that's happened since you pulled in here yesterday. I want you to write it all down—even the tiniest details, no matter how unimportant they seem."

"How long will that take?" Scoop asked. "We have a lot of other schools to go to. We're supposed to be in New Haven tomorrow."

"Then we'd best get busy," Officer Fallon said.

CHAPTER 5

Dink, Josh, and Ruth Rose watched the men follow Officer Fallon toward the police station. Above their heads, Tyrone's big plastic eyes stared.

"This is great," Dink grumbled. "Jud comes to see us, and his money gets stolen."

"I just don't see how anyone did it," Ruth Rose said. "We were all here yesterday afternoon, and Dean guarded Tyrone last night. Plus, he was locked inside Tyrone during the show."

"So maybe Dean is the thief," Josh said. "He could have taken the money last night or even during the show. No one saw what he did after that door closed."

"But we know what he did," Dink said. "He was working on the computer. Otherwise, Tyrone wouldn't have moved or talked."

"That's just it," Josh said. "Tyrone didn't move for the first few minutes, remember? Maybe that's when Dean was snitching the duffel bag!"

Dink shook his head. "I don't believe Dean would steal from his best friend," he said.

Just then Officer Keene pulled up in his cruiser. He climbed out with a roll of yellow tape and several wooden stakes in his arms. "Hi, kids," he said. "Little excitement, huh?"

He set the tape and stakes on the ground and walked over to Tyrone. The wedge was still in place, letting him open the door wider. He glanced inside.

"Whew, you could bake a pie in there," he said.

Officer Keene began shoving stakes into the ground around Tyrone. Then he strung the crime-scene tape around the stakes, forming a big circle around the dinosaur.

"Can we go to Ellie's?" Josh said. "My brain needs a drink."

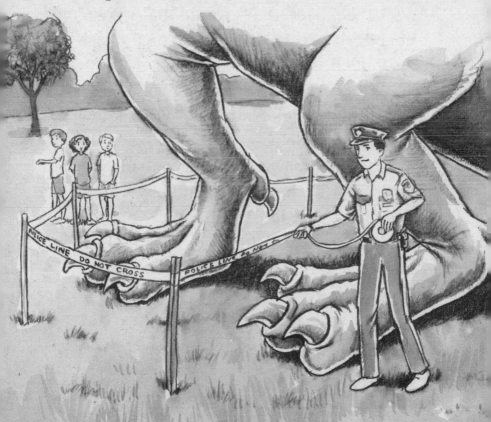

The kids started walking across Center Park.

"Do you really think Dean is the robber?" Ruth Rose asked Josh.

"Yes," he said. "He has a key, and he knew where the money was hidden."

"What about Scoop?" Ruth Rose asked. "Could he have borrowed a key from Dean or Jud?"

"If he had, they would have mentioned it to Officer Fallon," Josh responded.

"Maybe the thief was someone else," Dink said. "Some stranger who knew how to pick locks."

"But Dean was sleeping outside the dinosaur," Ruth Rose said. "How would a thief get past him?"

"That's why I think it's Dean," Josh said as he pulled open the door to Ellie's Diner.

The kids slid into a booth near the windows. One of the Tyrone flyers was taped to the glass. Ellie waved, then came over.

"Hi, kids. Why aren't you at the dinosaur show?" she asked.

"It's over," Josh said. "But someone stole their money!"

Ellie slid in next to Josh. "Who stole *whose* money?" she asked with wide eyes.

Ruth Rose explained about the money that was kept inside Tyrone's belly.

"Those poor guys," Ellie said, standing up. "They were so excited when they came in for breakfast this morning."

"Officer Fallon is on the case," Ruth Rose said.

"Good!" Ellie said. "Josh, your tongue is almost hanging out. How about some fresh lemonade?" she asked.

The kids agreed, and Ellie brought three tall glasses.

Josh took a big slurp through his

straw. "So, you guys agree that Dean is the robber?"

Dink stirred his lemonade. "I don't. Dean wouldn't be dumb enough to steal the money while he was guarding it last night," he said. "That would point the finger right at him."

Josh shook his head. "He could have taken the duffel bag during the show," he said.

"How?" Ruth Rose asked.

"Easy," Josh said. "He locks himself inside Tyrone. He moves the table and rug, grabs the duffel bag, then puts the rug and table back. It only takes him a minute."

"Then what?" Dink asked. "Where did he put the duffel bag?"

He and Ruth Rose stared at Josh, waiting for his answer.

Josh blinked at them. He took a sip of his lemonade. "Okay, here's what happened," he said. "Dean told us he built that little compartment inside Tyrone, right? So what if he built a second one that only he knows about? And *that's* where he hid the money!"

Dink looked at Josh over his glass. "You think the money is still inside Tyrone?"

"Why not?" Josh asked. "It's perfect. No one would think to look for it there."

Ruth Rose squinted her eyes at Josh. "Except someone with a sneaky mind like yours."

"I say we go search old Tyrone the T. rex," Josh said, finishing his lemonade. "If I'm right, Dean is planning to come and get the duffel bag as soon as he gets a chance."

"I hate to admit it, but Josh is making sense," Ruth Rose said. "It won't hurt to look inside Tyrone."

The kids left their money on the table, waved at Ellie, and headed back toward the high school.

A few minutes later, the kids stood looking at Tyrone surrounded by yellow crime-scene tape. Officer Keene was gone. "No one's supposed to go past the tape," Dink said.

"We could say we didn't see it," Josh suggested.

"Right," Dink said. "It's broad daylight and we can't see bright yellow tape."

"But what if it was dark?" Ruth Rose said, looking at Dink. "We could come back tonight."

Dink shook his head. "Forget it, guys. We'll be at the fireworks with our parents tonight."

Josh draped an arm around Dink's shoulder. "Perfect," he said. "While they're looking up at the sky, we can sneak away."

Dink finally agreed. "But I'm only doing this for Jud," he said.

The kids heard a bark and saw Mr.

Pocket and Randolph inspecting the rosebush in the park. They walked over to say hi.

"Did you hear about the robbery?" Ruth Rose asked.

"Yes, and I feel bad for those young men," Mr. Pocket said. "Any news?"

Dink shook his head.

"But something might break tonight," Josh said, giving Dink a little nudge.

"Our bush looks fine," Mr. Pocket said. "But I have to get rid of this dead one. Dink, you want to get the wheelbarrow for me?"

Dink ran to the shed. The wheelbarrow was where he had left it, leaning on the burlap bags. As Dink was leaving, he noticed muddy footprints on the bricks.

He brought the wheelbarrow to Mr. Pocket.

"Thanks," Mr. Pocket said as he

loaded the dead rosebush into the wheelbarrow. "I'll toss this into the school Dumpster." He walked away, with Randolph galloping along beside the wheelbarrow.

"Look, there's Jud and Scoop!" Josh said, pointing toward the dinosaur.

The two men were standing outside the crime-scene tape. Jud was talking and pointing a finger at the door in Tyrone's side. Scoop answered him, shaking his head.

The kids were too far away to hear their words. After a moment, the two men climbed into Scoop's car and drove away.

Dean wasn't with them.

"Officer Fallon must be holding Dean as a suspect," Dink said. The sweet lemonade in his stomach suddenly felt sour.

CHAPTER 6

As they walked home, the kids talked about the theft.

Josh stopped walking. A sly look shone from his green eyes. "I figured it out," he whispered. "I know who stole the money."

"Who?" Dink said.

"It was Tyrone!" Josh said. "While everyone was asleep, he walked to the bank and made a dino deposit!" Dink shoved Josh, and Ruth Rose rolled her eyes.

Before splitting up, they agreed to meet and walk to the fireworks together.

"Drop off your sleeping bags at my house," Dink said. "My folks said we could sleep outside after the fireworks."

"And wear dark clothes," Josh said.

At eight-thirty, Josh, Ruth Rose, and their families met at Dink's house. Dink, Josh, and Ruth Rose piled their sleeping bags on the picnic table. The adults carried blankets, bags of popcorn, and bug spray. Nate, Brian, and Bradley had each brought their favorite stuffed animals.

The three families walked to Main Street and turned left. They took another left at Holly's Gas Station. From there it was only a short walk down East Green Street to the swimming pool, where the fireworks were set up.

"Why are you three dressed in black?" Ruth Rose's dad asked. "You look like ninjas."

"We're hoping the mosquitoes won't

see us in the dark," Ruth Rose said, glancing at Dink.

Dink, Josh, and Ruth Rose walked ahead, leaving the others behind.

"Good thinking," Josh said when he was sure he couldn't be overheard.

A few minutes later, they all arrived at the town pool. Hundreds of people were already there. Blankets and chairs covered the lawns near the pool, tennis courts, and baseball field.

The fire truck was parked nearby in case it was needed.

"I see Jud, Scoop, and Dean," Josh said. The three men sat leaning against the fence that surrounded the baseball field. "Let's go sit with them."

"We can't," Ruth Rose said. "If we do, they'll see us sneak away later."

"Well, let's at least go over and say hi," Dink said.

"Yeah, and we can see if Dean looks guilty," Josh commented.

The kids wove their way through the blankets and chairs. Jud noticed them first and stood up.

"Howdy," he said, waving. "You guys want to sit with us?" Scoop and Dean said hi, too, but didn't stand up.

"Can't," Josh said. "We have to stay near our parents."

"Officer Fallon is a nice guy," Jud said. "I sure hope he can find our money. We're taking Tyrone down tomorrow and leaving."

"Where are you going?" Ruth Rose asked.

"New Haven first, then a bunch of other towns," Scoop said. "We have a lot more money to earn."

Dean didn't join the conversation. His dark eyes stared straight ahead.

"Good evening," a voice said. It was Mr. Linkletter, the Shangri-la Hotel's manager. He was sitting on a lawn chair a few feet away. Everyone said hi.

"I hope your room is comfortable," Mr. Linkletter said to Jud and Scoop.

"It's great," Jud answered.

Just then a circle of blue light lit the sky over their heads. "Oooh!" cried hundreds of people.

"They're starting!" Ruth Rose said. "We'd better go find our parents."

"How about breakfast at Ellie's tomorrow?" Jud asked. "I don't want to leave without saying good-bye."

"Sure," Dink said. "What time?"

"We're getting up real early to load Tyrone onto the truck," he said. "So how about nine o'clock?"

"We'll be there," said Dink. The kids walked away toward their families. They picked a spot near the tennis courts where they could still keep an eye on the three men by the fence.

"Guys, did you hear what Jud said?" Ruth Rose asked. "They're taking Tyrone apart tomorrow!"

"So if that's where Dean hid the money, he needs to get it before then," Josh said.

"Or whoever," Dink added.

"Trust me, it's Dean," Josh went on. "Did you guys notice how he just sat and didn't say a word to anyone? In my book, that spells G-U-I-L-T-Y."

Volunteer firefighters had built a low barricade around the fireworks. The police had placed detour signs on River Road to keep cars away. Firefighters in white T-shirts went through the crowd, handing out tiny American flags.

For a few minutes the kids watched fireworks bursting over their heads. The sky went from black to red, white, and blue. The crowd clapped and whistled and yelled.

"When the next really big one goes off, let's boogie," Josh whispered.

A second later, the sky blossomed

into a giant yellow flower. While every eye was looking up, Dink, Josh, and Ruth Rose slipped away in the dark.

They darted across East Green Street and raced to the high school lawns.

A nearly full moon cast the dinosaur's shadow halfway across the playing field. Behind the kids, the sky was still lit with fireworks. A breeze swept across the field, making the yellow tape rattle against the stakes.

"Now what?" Dink asked. "I really don't like being here, guys."

"I don't, either," Ruth Rose said. "But if the duffel bag is still inside Tyrone, we have to find it tonight!"

CHAPTER 7

"Let's just do it," Josh said. "It'll take us five minutes. If we don't find the money, we go back to watch the fireworks."

The kids crept under the yellow tape. They were concealed in Tyrone's dark shadow. The rubber wedge was holding the door open an inch. Josh removed it and swung the door open.

"I can't see anything!" Dink said. "How can we search in the dark?"

"Wait," Ruth Rose said. She pulled a small flashlight from her pocket. She flipped it on and aimed the beam past the folded steps, into Tyrone's belly.

The table and rug were still off to one side. The compartment lid was up, and the space was still empty. Then Ruth Rose shut off the light.

Dink pulled down the steps, and they scrambled up into Tyrone's belly. Dink folded the steps back while Josh eased the door shut.

They were in a dark, stuffy cave.

"It's roasting in here!" Josh's voice complained from the darkness.

Dink was on his knees. One arm rested against the small table. The compartment that once held the duffel bag was in front of him, but he couldn't see it.

"Let's get this over with," Dink said. "I'd like to get back to the fireworks before my folks know we're gone."

Ruth Rose flipped on her flashlight

and shone it around the small space. "Okay, Josh, show us this secret hiding place," she said.

"It wouldn't be right out in plain sight," Josh said. "Look for someplace no one would think of."

On his knees, Josh shuffled around to face the rear legs. They were attached to the rest of the body with large bolts. "I'll bet these legs are hollow," he said.

Josh felt around and, sure enough, was able to stick his arm down inside one leg. "Nothing down there," he said.

Dink examined the other leg, but there was nothing hidden inside that one, either.

"What about up inside his head?" Ruth Rose asked. Her light followed the cables up Tyrone's chest and neck. At the top, only a dark hole showed where the head was.

"Let's find out," Dink said. He stood up and tried to reach his hand up to

Tyrone's head cavity. "I'm not tall enough."

"Wait a sec," Josh said. He lifted the laptop computer off the table and set it on the floor. Then he slid the table over to Dink.

Dink climbed onto the table and reached again. This time his arm was inside Tyrone's head. He moved his hand around in the space. "All I feel are the wires that come from the computer," he said. "But my arm isn't long enough to reach all the way."

"Could I fit in there?" Ruth Rose asked.

"Probably," Dink said. "The head is hollow."

Josh giggled. "Like yours," he said.

"Let me go up," Ruth Rose said. "I'll stand on the table, then you guys boost me."

Ruth Rose and Dink traded places. Josh held the flashlight in his mouth as he and Dink lifted Ruth Rose up Tyrone's throat. She disappeared into the head, with only her feet sticking out. Then her feet vanished and they saw her face peering down at them.

"There's nothing up here but a little speaker attached to those wires," she said. "And a bunch of teeth."

Josh flashed the light around the walls. "I don't see anyplace else you could hide a pile of money," he said.

"So what should we do?" Dink asked.

"First, get some air in here," Josh said. He handed Dink the flashlight and reached for the door.

Dink shut off the flashlight. "Don't open it too wide," he said. "I don't feel like getting arrested for breaking and entering a dinosaur!"

Josh shoved the door. It didn't move. "Help me, Dinkus. It's stuck."

Both boys leaned their shoulders against the door and pushed.

"The door must have locked when we closed it," Josh said. "We forgot to wedge it open with that rubber thing!"

Dink flipped on the flashlight and aimed the beam up at Ruth Rose. "If I hand this to you, can you shine it out through the mouth?" he asked. "If you yell, someone might hear you."

She shook her head. "The mouth is closed."

"We have to try something," Dink said, waving the flashlight around. "I'm not staying in here all night!"

"Got it," Josh said. "I think I know how to boot up Dean's computer. If I can make Tyrone's mouth open, we can yell for help through the microphone and speaker."

"No one would hear us over the fireworks noise," Ruth Rose said. "But you gave me another idea, Josh. If you can open Tyrone's mouth, maybe I can climb out that way!"

"Ruth Rose, Tyrone's head is too high off the ground," Dink said.

He looked at Josh. "Is there anything we can make a ladder out of?"

Suddenly Josh grabbed the flashlight from Dink's hand. He shone it around the walls until the beam fell on the row of hooks. "I thought so," Josh said.

"What?" Dink said.

Josh reached out and grabbed a coil of rope. "This," he said. "We can use it to lower Ruth Rose out Tyrone's mouth to the ground!"

Dink looked up at Ruth Rose. "Do you think you could?" he asked.

Ruth Rose nodded. "Tyrone's mouth is pretty big," she said.

"Like Josh's," Dink said, grinning at his friend.

"Very amusing," Josh said. He passed

the flashlight to Dink, then sat in front of the laptop. He turned it on, then tapped a few keys.

Several icons appeared on the screen. One of them was labeled TYRONE. Josh clicked on it, and a window appeared showing a list of choices. One of the words was MOUTH.

"Bingo," Josh said. "Get ready, Ruth Rose!"

Josh clicked on MOUTH. A second later, Dink heard a grinding sound.

"It worked!" Ruth Rose yelled. "Tyrone's mouth is opening!"

CHAPTER 8

Dink set the flashlight on the floor and tied one end of the rope to the folding steps. Josh formed a loop in the other end, big enough for Ruth Rose to step in. He stood on the table and handed her the loop.

"Are you sure you want to do this?" Dink asked.

"It'll be easy," Ruth Rose said. "I climb down the rope ladder from my cousin's tree house all the time."

"We'll hold the rope till you're ready to go down," Josh said. He added,

"Be careful of those teeth!"

"Okay, give me a minute." Ruth Rose's face disappeared. Some of the slack rope went with her. "All right!" she yelled. "Just lower me real slow."

The boys felt the rope tighten with Ruth Rose's weight. They let the rope slip slowly through their fingers. Dink felt the friction making his palms burn.

Then the rope went totally slack.

"Is she down?" Josh asked.

They both heard someone banging on the door in Tyrone's side. "I'll be right back!" Ruth Rose yelled.

Dink and Josh sat and leaned against a curved wall. Ruth Rose's flashlight was growing dim, so Dink shut it off.

"Wish this place had an air conditioner," Josh said after a minute. He wiped sweat off his face with his T-shirt.

"Why not wish for a full refrigerator while you're at it," Dink said.

Josh grinned. "Or a microwave and a pizza. But I'd settle for a big fan."

The boys sat in the dark. Dink felt sweat trickling into his eyes.

"I'm cooking," Josh moaned.

"Don't be such a baby," Dink said. "Imagine what it would be like inside a *real* Tyrannosaurus!"

Josh giggled in the dark. "Did dinosaurs eat kids?" he asked.

"No, Josh, because humans didn't live then," Dink said. "Besides, if a T. rex got one taste of you, he'd spit you out."

Josh poked Dink in the ribs.

Dink poked him back.

Just as Josh put a wrestling hold around Dink's neck, they heard something thump outside.

Josh gulped. "Do you suppose it's Dean, coming to get the money?"

Dink crawled to the door and put his ear against it. The door opened, and

Dink nearly fell on top of Jud. Behind Jud stood Officer Fallon and Ruth Rose.

"You sure get yourself in some pickles," Officer Fallon said, shining his flashlight in Dink's eyes. "Good thing I found Jud at the fireworks."

Jud lowered the steps so Dink and Josh could climb down to the ground.

"Thanks," Josh said. "We were melting in there!"

"I don't suppose you found the money," Jud said. "Ruth Rose told us what you were up to."

Dink shook his head. "Sorry," he said.

"I'm afraid that whoever took that duffel bag disappeared with it," Officer Fallon said.

Jud nodded. "It must have happened last night after we went to bed," he said. "I just don't see how."

Officer Fallon shined his light at the

ground. "It rained last night, so even if the crook left footprints, they'd have washed away."

Footprints, Dink thought. "I saw wet footprints in that garden shed," he said. Dink pointed through the darkness toward the rose garden. "I went in to get the wheelbarrow for Mr. Pocket."

"That means someone went in there after it rained," Ruth Rose said. "And that was in the middle of the night!"

"Maybe the footprints were left by our thief," Officer Fallon said. He put a hand on Dink's shoulder. "Show me."

Dink led the way across the dark lawn. "There it is," he said when they reached the small garden shed.

"You folks please stay out here," Officer Fallon told Josh, Ruth Rose, and Jud. His flashlight beam found the screwdriver. He removed it and opened the door. He played the light over the floor. Dried muddy footprints led from the door to the back of the shed.

"Hold this for me," Officer Fallon said, handing his flashlight to Dink. "Stand by the door so I have light."

Officer Fallon stepped inside and kneeled to examine the footprints. Then he walked through the shed, checking inside, under, and behind anything large enough to hide a person.

At the back of the shed, he moved the wheelbarrow. He poked at the stack of burlap sacks with a toe. Then he peeled off several of the bags and set them on the floor.

Dink saw him bend over and pull something from under the remaining bags.

"Jud, would you come in here?" Officer Fallon yelled.

Jud stuck his head in the door.

"Is this what you've been looking for?"

Officer Fallon was holding a dark

brown duffel bag. It was fat, as if stuffed with something. A long zipper ran along one side.

Jud beamed. "You found it!" he said.

Officer Fallon carried the bag out of the shed and set it on the ground. Under the flashlight beam, he pulled open the zipper. Nearly filling the bag were thousands of dollar bills bound in rubber bands.

Officer Fallon looked up at Jud. "Is this your money?" he asked.

Jud nodded. "I hope it's all there."

"What's that?" Dink asked. He

pointed to something pale green that was stuck to the side of the canvas duffel.

"It's a Band-Aid," Ruth Rose said.

"Don't touch," Officer Fallon cautioned. He pulled a small plastic bag from his pocket. Using the point of his pen, he knocked the Band-Aid into the baggie, then sealed it.

"I wonder who this came from," Officer Fallon said. He held his light on the plastic bag.

"Scoop put on a Band-Aid like that one yesterday," Ruth Rose said. "He burned his finger on his car radiator."

"I saw one on Dean's finger, too," Josh said.

"We all use them," Jud said. He reached into a pocket of his jeans and pulled out a green Band-Aid.

Officer Fallon held Jud's flat Band-Aid next to the used one in his baggie. The two Band-Aids were the same.

CHAPTER 9

"All three of you fellas wear these Band-Aids?" Officer Fallon asked Jud.

Jud nodded. "Working on Tyrone, we were always nicking our fingers," he said. "So I bought a box of Band-Aids, and we all keep a few in our pocket."

Officer Fallon glanced at the duffel bag. "Who handled that bag last?"

"I'm the only one who ever put the money in the bag," Jud said. "I must've been wearing a Band-Aid, and it slipped off my finger when I stuck the bag in the compartment."

"Or the Band-Aid could have fallen off the thief's finger when he stole the bag," Officer Fallon said. "Whoever it was." He gave Jud a close look.

Jud thought for a moment before he spoke. "I know it looks like one of us stole the money," he said. "But *I* sure didn't take it, and I can't believe Dean or Scoop would, either!"

"Could the robber be someone else?" Dink asked.

"But who?" Officer Fallon said. "Jud, you told me only you and Dean have keys to your dinosaur."

"That's right," Jud said. "But Dean is my best friend!"

Officer Fallon slipped the baggie and his pen into a pocket. "Between Scoop Raker and Dean Whitefeather, who had more opportunity to get at that duffel bag?" he asked Jud.

Jud looked at his feet. "Dean, I

guess," he mumbled. "He slept next to Tyrone last night."

Officer Fallon put his hand on Jud's shoulder. "I want you to wait in my office while I get Dean," he said. "Do you think he's still at the fireworks?"

"I guess," Jud said.

"Meanwhile, I'll put this money in our safe," Officer Fallon went on. "I'll see you at the station in a few minutes."

Looking embarrassed, Jud turned and headed toward Main Street. In a few seconds, he had disappeared in the darkness.

Officer Fallon looked at Dink, Josh, and Ruth Rose. "Your parents might be missing you by now," he said. "I'll take you back, okay?"

Dink, Josh, and Ruth Rose followed Officer Fallon to his cruiser and climbed into the backseat. Officer Fallon drove them to Main Street.

Colorful fireworks were still lighting

the skies over the town swimming pool. Officer Fallon parked between the tennis courts and the baseball field.

The kids watched him walk toward the baseball field fence; then they went to find their parents.

"There you are!" Dink's mother said. "We thought you'd been abducted by aliens!" Looking at his watch, Dink realized they'd been gone nearly half an hour.

The kids sat where they could watch Officer Fallon. He walked over to Dean, and the two men stood talking for a minute. Then Officer Fallon led Dean to his cruiser. The car pulled onto Main Street and disappeared.

"I can't believe Jud's friend robbed him," Ruth Rose said.

Josh lay back on the grass. "I wonder what will happen to Tyrone now," he said.

"I guess Jud and Scoop will hire

someone to take Dean's place," Dink said.

"Where is Scoop?" Ruth Rose asked.

"Wasn't he by the fence with Dean?" Dink asked.

"No," Josh said. "Only Dean was there. Maybe Scoop went back to the hotel. He said he didn't get much sleep last night because of the storm."

Dink remembered the storm raging outside his window last night. He thought about Dean waking up in the rain and dashing for the truck. In his mind, he saw those muddy footprints on the shed floor. And that morning, Scoop's wet sneakers hanging from his car antenna.

"Guys, I think everyone's wrong about Dean!" Dink said suddenly. "I think Scoop stole the money, and I think *he* hid it in the garden shed!"

"But he didn't have a key," Josh said.

"I think Scoop knew that Dean wouldn't sleep outside once it started to rain. Dean moved into the truck cab to stay dry, and that's when Scoop got inside Tyrone."

"How? Scoop didn't have a key," Josh said again.

"Somehow, Scoop must have taken Jud's key while Jud was asleep," Dink said. "Scoop stole the duffel bag, hid it in the shed, then ran back to the hotel. He must have planned to return to the shed later to get the money."

Suddenly Ruth Rose gasped. "Maybe that's where Scoop is now!" she said. "He could sneak away, like we did!"

"Come on!" Dink said. The kids zipped past the Mystic Greenhouse, cut behind the Book Nook, and raced toward the rose garden. Out of breath, they crouched behind some rosebushes ten yards from the shed. A light flickered through the open door.

"Someone's inside!" Josh hissed.

The three kids crept close enough to

see inside the shed. They saw a dark-haired figure kneeling in front of the stack of burlap bags. When the man stood up, they knew it was Scoop Raker.

"What should we do?" Ruth Rose whispered.

"The screwdriver is there," Josh said. "I'm gonna lock him in!"

"No!" Dink said. "Let's go get Officer Fallon!"

Josh shook his head. "Not enough time! When Scoop doesn't find the money, he'll take off!" He started to crawl through the rosebushes toward the shed. "Ouch!" he yelled.

"What happened?" whispered Ruth Rose.

"Darn thorns!" Josh whispered back.

Suddenly Scoop burst out of the shed. He turned his flashlight beam on Josh. Before anyone else could react, Scoop had grabbed Josh by the arm.

"Okay, kid, what did you do with the money?" he demanded.

"YOU LEAVE HIM ALONE!" Ruth Rose cried as she and Dink sprinted to Josh's side.

"Yes, leave him alone," a deeper voice said. Officer Fallon and Dean stepped out from behind the shed.

CHAPTER 10

An hour later, the kids were lying on their sleeping bags in Dink's backyard. They were gazing up at the stars.

"There's the Big Dipper!" Josh said, sitting up.

"I think I see Mars!" Dink said.

"There's a shooting star. Make a wish!" Ruth Rose said. "I wish I could be the first woman president!"

"I wish Ruth Rose could become president and put me in charge of desserts," Josh said.

Dink and Ruth Rose sat up and laughed.

"I wish Jud and Dean would leave Tyrone in Green Lawn," Dink said.

"Yeah," Josh said. "That would be so excellent. We could make him walk all over town."

"People would pay us to give them rides in Tyrone," Ruth Rose added. "We could send the money to Jud and Dean for their museum."

The three kids sighed and settled back on their sleeping bags.

"I still can't figure out how Scoop got Jud's key," Ruth Rose said.

"Oh, that was easy," Josh said. "I figured it out a long time ago."

Dink popped up and glared at his friend. "And are you planning to *tell* us?"

Josh let out a dramatic sigh. "Scoop heard Dean say it was going to rain last night. He knew Dean would probably move inside somewhere to stay dry. I think that's when Scoop decided to steal the money. He waited till Jud was sound asleep, then took his key."

"But how did Scoop get into Jud's room?" Dink asked.

"He didn't have to," Josh said. "They slept in the same room."

"Joshua, how do you know that?" Ruth Rose asked.

Josh grinned. "Remember when Mr. Linkletter said hi to us at the fireworks? I heard him ask Jud and Scoop how their room was. Room, not rooms."

"It's a good thing Officer Fallon showed up at the shed," Dink said. "I wonder how he knew Scoop would go there."

"Dean might have convinced him," Josh said. "Dean must've figured out the only way the crook could have gotten a key was by taking it from Jud during the night. And Dean knew Jud and Scoop shared a room."

"Well, I hate to admit it," Dink said, "but you're pretty smart."

"I know," Josh said. "But thanks anyway."

"You're welcome," Dink said.

"Maybe I'll put you in charge of the FBI when I'm president," Ruth Rose said.

Josh yawned. "Naw. I'd rather be in charge of food."

The three kids smiled in the dark. Then, as the stars twinkled above them, they slowly went to sleep.

About the Author

Ron Roy is the author of more than thirty-five books for children, including *A Thousand Pails of Water*, *Where's Buddy?*, and the award-winning *Whose Hat Is That?* When he's not writing a thrilling new story for the A to Z Mysteries® series, Ron spends time traveling all over the country and restoring his old Connecticut farmhouse.

Collect clues with Dink, Josh, and Ruth Rose
in their next exciting adventure,

THE UNWILLING UMPIRE

"You're not going to believe this!" Josh
whispered. "Mr. Pocket's autographed
baseballs are gone!"

"What do you mean, gone?" Dink
asked.

"I mean they're not there anymore!"
Josh yelped.

Ruth Rose looked toward the club-
house. "Maybe Mr. Pocket moved them
someplace else when the game started,"
she said.

Josh was shaking his head. "No! The
glass case is smashed in a million
pieces!" he said. "Someone stole those
balls!"

www 15 tv - net

Pasarela espo mis xx
años 6